PAW PATROL™

This edition published by Parragon Books Ltd in 2018

Parragon Books Ltd
Chartist House
15–17 Trim Street
Bath BA1 1HA, UK
www.parragon.com

Adapted by Mickie Matheis
Based on the teleplay "Pups Save a School Bus" by Andrew Guerdat
Illustrated by Fabrizio Petrossi

ISBN 978-1-4748-9821-8

T#591938

Printed in China

PUPS SAVE
A SCHOOL BUS

PaRragon

Bath • New York • Cologne • Melbourne • Delhi
Hong Kong • Shenzhen • Singapore

One sunny morning, Mr. Hudson the school bus driver was starting his route through Adventure Bay.

Suddenly, Mr. Porter's delivery truck spilled a big bunch of bananas! The bananas landed in front of the school bus, sending it sliding and skidding off the road.

There were loud popping sounds as the bus rolled over some pointy spikes!

All four tyres on the bus were flat!
How could Mr. Hudson pick up the children
and take them to school? He knew he had
to alert the PAW Patrol!

"Don't worry," Ryder said. "No job is too big, no pup is too small!"
Ryder called all the pups to the PAW Patroller.

Inside the PAW Patroller, Ryder told the team about the four flat tyres.

"Rocky, your ratchet and tyre-patching gear will get that bus rolling again. Marshall, use your water cannons to spray the squished fruit off the street so no one else skids on it."

"But how will the children get to school on time?" Chase asked. The bell was going to ring in ten minutes!

Ryder thought for a moment. "We'll just have to use a substitute school bus — the PAW Patroller!" The pups cheered as they raced to the scene.

Rocky used his forklift to prop up the bus. Then he got to work removing the tyres with his ratchet.

At the same time, Marshall hosed down the mush on the road with his water cannons.
"Wow!" exclaimed Mr. Hudson. "That's one power-washing pup!"

Meanwhile, Ryder, Chase and Robo Dog used the PAW Patroller to pick up the children and take them to school. At the first stop was their friend, Alex.

"This isn't a school bus — it's a *cool* bus!" he said as he got on.

Next, they picked up Julius and Julia.
"Come aboard the temporary bus!" Chase announced over his loudspeaker.
The brother and sister hurried inside and sat down.

Then they came to a stop where a little girl stood with Mayor Goodway and her pet chicken, Chickaletta.

"Oh, look — a new school bus!" said Mayor Goodway.

Chickaletta was so excited that she dropped her corn, and it rolled away. She immediately ran after it.

Ryder, Robo Dog and Chase followed closely behind her.

The older children explored the PAW Patroller.
Alex climbed into Chase's police truck, Julius
pretended to steer Zuma's hovercraft, and Julia sat in
Rubble's rig.
Ryder, Chase and Robo Dog finally returned with
Chickaletta, who had picked up her corn.

Chickaletta started to peck at the PAW Patroller's control panel. Then they heard a rumbling noise....

One by one, the pups' vehicles rolled out onto the road — with the children inside! Chickaletta had pressed the launch button with her beak!

"Whoa!" yelled Alex.
"Whee!" screamed Julia.
"Woo-hoo!" whooped Julius.

"No, Chickaletta!" said Ryder. But the poor chicken was so startled that she flew straight up, landed in Skye's helicopter, and pecked the control panel there, too!

The helicopter's engine started, and away the chicken flew!

Ryder quickly called the other pups at the Lookout. "Team," he said, "our school bus rescue has taken a detour! The children are out riding in your vehicles! We need to get them back."

Skye popped open the wings on her Pup Pack and zoomed up to the chicken flying in her helicopter.

"Looks like you need a copilot," she said, slipping into the seat next to Chickaletta.

Skye grabbed the controller and safely steered the chopper and its pecking passenger towards home.

Back on the ground, Rubble raced towards his rig on his skateboard. With a few fancy moves, he flipped himself inside the Digger next to Julia. He pressed the brake, barely avoiding a crash with Mr. Porter's fruit stand.

Out on the water, Julius was speeding towards Cap'n Turbot's boat in the hovercraft. Zuma whizzed alongside on a kite-powered surfboard and leaped behind the wheel.

The hovercraft turned, missing the boat at the last second!

Meanwhile, Ryder and Chase caught up with Alex. "Time to pull over," the pup barked. But Alex didn't know how!

Ryder instructed Chase to shoot a net from his Pup Pack. The net sailed through the air and stretched between two trees, catching the patrol truck like a football.

"Goal!" Ryder and Chase shouted, high-fiving each other.

Everyone rushed back to the PAW Patroller. If they hurried, they could still get the children to school on time!

But then the PAW Patroller's door suddenly opened, and a little girl threw out a bouncy ball. Robo Dog chased it while the girl started up the giant vehicle. The PAW Patroller rolled down the street!

Ryder sprang into action.

"Skye, get your helicopter back in the air and lower the harness!" he said.

Once Ryder had strapped himself into the harness, Skye flew over the PAW Patroller. Ryder dropped down through the roof and ran to the front. He reached for the controls . . .

. . . and stopped the vehicle in front of the school just as the other pups arrived.

The children waved goodbye and ran inside as the school bus rumbled up the street. Rocky had fixed the tyres, and the bus was as good as new!

"Did you just get here?" he asked his teammates with a giggle. "What took you so long?"

THE END!